Left Hand Black

American Depraved: Book Two

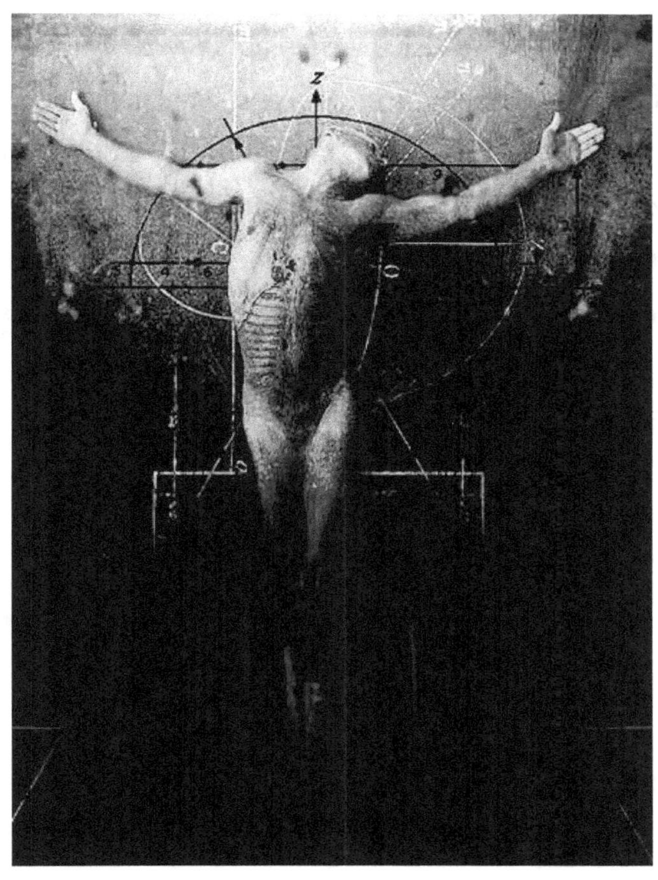

Jeffrey Abney

Dedication

To my Grandmother who introduced me to murderers and monsters through her book collection. She had no idea it would spark a lifelong passion.

About The Author

A father of three, a disabled veteran of the United States Army, and a practicing attorney living in St. Louis, Missouri. A lifelong fan of horror and psychological thrillers, and a lifelong aspiring author.

Chapter 1

Oriole crush

The remnants of the evening sun cast a warm glow over Baltimore, drawing out colors in the city that had long lain dormant. The man stood on the balcony of his rented row house, a humble façade that hid hidden depths, much like himself. He took in the scent of salt from the nearby harbor mixed with the faint whiff of fried food wafting from a bustling diner down the street. The familiar pulse of life energized him, each laugh and shout below resonating with deliberate purpose.

He adjusted his collar, smoothing the fabric as he surveyed the neighborhood, which was a vibrant tapestry stitched together by contrasting stories. The thrill of displacement vibrated in his veins. Here was a canvas awaiting his artistry. The FBI agent was due to arrive soon, and he could almost taste the tension threading through the air like static before a storm.

His fingers absentmindedly traced the patterns on the railing, feeling the rough grain beneath his skin. He imagined how it would feel to mold fate through careful selection and precise execution.

Cole's transfer had come sooner than he anticipated, thrilling him in ways he couldn't quite articulate. He worked his way downstairs and stepped into the thrumming heart of the Inner Harbor, feeling the familiar rhythms of Baltimore pulse through him like a heartbeat, every street corner resonating with a promise of new beginnings. He breathed in the rich, salty air mingled with the scent of roasted coffee from a nearby café, each whiff invigorating his senses.

As he settled into his new surroundings, the city whispered secrets of its past, layers of history wrapped tightly within its neighborhoods. The vibrant colors and bustling sounds masked an undercurrent of tension that intrigued him; crime had a way of curling into the shadows where good intentions faltered. He watched people move about their lives, their faces revealing stories—pain, joy, fear—all woven together by the fabric of urban existence.

His thoughts drifted back to St. Louis, where he had carefully analyzed every move Cole Hunter had made. The agent's rise was predictable; ambition radiated from him like heat from concrete in the summer sun. To an outsider, Cole appeared resolute and unyielding, but he knew better. He understood that beneath that polished exterior lay a mind constantly seeking patterns, forever searching for answers in the chaos.

Now that Cole was here in Baltimore, the thrill of the hunt awaited him. The city's pulse thrummed beneath his skin as he navigated its winding streets, a maze of brick and asphalt that whispered forgotten secrets. The sun dipped low in the west, casting long shadows that danced along row houses and alleyways. He slowed his pace outside a small café, his eyes brushing over the patrons gathered at tables on the sidewalk. He couldn't help but admire their ignorance as they enjoyed their drinks, blissfully unaware of the darkness that lurked just over their shoulders.

When he had arrived in Baltimore, he had settled into a routine, a familiar choreography that brought him a sense of calm and control. It had not taken long for him to find his new target. His rented row house was now riddled with scattered notes and photographs of the target and his loved ones. The target's life was about to unravel in the most delightful of ways. The detailed notes captured the minutiae of the target's life, down to the minute. The target's routines were so entrenched that it made orchestrating the murders to come almost too easy.

The target was a finance manager at a local firm, and he had that unremarkable face that most people overlooked. The killer found no beauty in the mundane life his target had chosen, but the target's level of blandness did fascinate him. This target would carry no weight in the memory of those who passed him on the street: perfectly ordinary, just another face in the crowd.

The first step after selecting a target was always intense observation. He would immerse himself in every facet of the target's life. Public records were such a font of useful information. The second step would be to observe the target's loved ones and familiarize himself with their routines and habits. The final step was to plan each and every kill down to the last detail. He was an artist, after all. These people were to become his instruments, and Baltimore was to become the canvas.

The only decision he had not made yet was how many bodies he should drop in the city this time around.

Chapter 2
1970

The sun hung low over Baltimore, casting a warm golden hue that clung to the air, mingling with the scent of popcorn and roasted peanuts wafting from nearby vendors. Cole Hunter stood at the edge of Oriole Park at Camden Yards, where a palpable excitement vibrated through the crowd, a stark contrast to the grim investigations normally weighing on his shoulders. The sounds of cheering fans filled his ears, the crack of a bat connecting with a ball resonating like a heartbeat for the city.

He watched as families cheered in the crowd, children clutching foam fingers and parents chatting animatedly about the season's ups and downs. For a moment, he allowed himself to get lost in their joy, this city alive with hope, buoyed by the Orioles' chase for glory. It brought back memories of the last pennant chase he had watched when his Cardinals won it all during his first year on the job. This year's incarnation of the Orioles had three of the best pitchers in the game: Palmer, McNally, and Cuellar. If they were going to win it all, those three star pitchers would be the driving force behind them.

He focused on the game, but the numbers on the scoreboard blurred as his mind drifted. The Orioles were in prime form that season, led by their star pitcher, Jim Palmer, a man whose reputation for precision mirrored Cole's own professional ethos. Palmer's mastery on the mound had earned him accolades, and as he threw pitch after pitch, Cole couldn't help but think about patterns. The way each player moved in sync, how strategies unfolded like crime scenes, the meticulous planning to outmaneuver an opponent.

Cole had cemented his reputation as a rising star in the FBI early on. The success of capturing El Pinatero, the maniac who had slaughtered three people and played with their organs as if they were silly putty, had instantly put him on the radar with the top brass. It didn't hurt that his partner wanted no credit and retired soon after.

The six years that followed were spent primarily solving mafia-related murders and refining his investigative skills. The few murders that came across his desk were typically one-off crimes of passion or the occasional money-related killing. What got him his promotion, though, was discovering who was behind a string of bank robberies in St. Louis in the winter of 1969. He had gotten lucky when one of the gang's friends was caught for grand theft auto and wanted to cut a deal to face lesser charges. It turned out he was close with the gang's talkative getaway driver. After some surveillance, they quickly determined the next bank job and organized a sting operation that replaced all of the employees that day with agents or local police. The moment the gang entered and drew their weapons, a dozen guns were drawn on them and their exit was sealed.

Director Shehbazski had been sad to see the transfer papers cross his desk, but he knew it was best for Cole's career and didn't put up a fight on the transfer to the East Coast. Cole, a St. Louis native, would have normally been against the transfer. But his ambition, and his girlfriend, had him looking on the positive side of things immediately. His girlfriend, Shayla, was from Maryland and she was as excited as could be about returning home to be near her family.

It had been a crisp autumn evening when Cole first met Shayla, the air thick with the scent of damp leaves on the ground. An art exhibit featuring local photographers had drawn him into a crowded gallery in the Forest Park area. He had intended to immerse himself in the work, to analyze the shadows and light captured by different lenses, but instead found himself drawn to her laughter, bright and cutting through the chatter.

Shayla stood in front of a striking portrait, her black hair catching the light as she tilted her head in curiosity. He remembered how her fingers brushed against the frame almost reverently, as if trying to decipher the story within the image. Her work as a nurse gave her a unique perspective, one more empathetic than most. He noted the subtle grace with which she spoke to those around her, making everyone feel as if they were important, even in a room full of strangers.

As she moved through the crowd, her dark curls bounced playfully with each step. Cole had been drawn to her energy, the way she engaged people with genuine interest. Approaching her had almost felt like stepping off a ledge into unknown waters. Their conversation began with small talk, but they had spoken for hours that night, exchanging thoughts on art and life while sipping white wine.

That had been six months ago, and they had been engrossed in each other ever since. When he told her about the transfer, she was thrilled and began making plans immediately for him to meet all of her old friends and family. She also started making lists of places he just had to visit in Baltimore.

All in all, life was coming together nicely for Cole. His career was progressing in the right direction, his romantic life was on track, and he might even get a chance to experience another baseball World Series run. How could things possibly get any better?

Chapter 3

The Left Hand of God

Director Johnson was a stout man with a no-nonsense demeanor that demanded attention. The sharp lines of his suit complemented the hardness of his features as he leaned forward, hands clasped and resting on the desk. "Cole," he began in a voice that resonated with authority, "you're stepping into a significant role here."

Cole nodded, absorbing the words like a sponge but also processing every detail around him: the sterile white walls adorned with motivational posters, the fluorescent lights casting a harsh glare on the polished conference table, and the faint smell of stale coffee lingering in the air.

Before him was his new boss, Director Jack Johnson. "Welcome aboard, Agent Hunter," he said, his voice steady and clipped. Cole practiced a measured response, though Director Johnson's presence certainly knotted his stomach.

Beside Director Johnson stood his new partner, Joanne Misko. She provided a striking contrast to Johnson's rigidity. She had an easy smile that seemed genuine but carried an edge Cole couldn't quite decipher. With a slight nod she said, "Looking forward to working together. I hope you bring some of your St. Louis luck to Charm City."

"Charm City?" Cole responded, tilting his head in mild confusion.

Joanne's smile widened. "No one told you? Baltimore is called Charm City—probably because of all the charming citizens that fill this place." Director Johnson grunted in what Cole assumed was his form of a chuckle, then handed Joanne a piece of paper from his desk. "You've already caught your first case. Here is the address. The local police are on the scene. Don't let them give you any trouble about jurisdiction. If you determine it is within our purview, assert our authority."

***

The metallic scent of blood tinged the air, a lingering reminder of violence that clawed at Cole's throat. He stepped closer to the body, his eyes drawn to the stark contrast of black ink against pale skin. The victim's hand rested unnaturally on her neck, fingers splayed as if caught in a desperate attempt to escape. Each detail screamed for attention, a whisper of horror echoing in the back of his mind.

Cole crouched down, feeling the rough asphalt beneath him, cool and unyielding. The scene was so quiet, you could hear the distant hum of Baltimore's daily life melding into a muted backdrop as he focused on the body before him.

The victim's face was frozen in an expression of terror; it was a haunting mask that seemed to mock him, daring him to unearth the truth. He couldn't shake the chill running down his spine; it was a visceral response that threatened to drown out his professional resolve. He swallowed hard, forcing down the bile that rose. The methodical precision of this act gnawed at his gut. This wasn't just a killing; this was someone playing out a fantasy.

He forced himself closer, examining every intricate detail of the scene. Joanne stood across from him, her skin a noticeable green shade. The victim's skin was pale, almost ghostly in contrast to the thick black ink that had seeped into her left hand — a striking mark against her flesh.

Cole's fingers brushed the raised texture of the ink as he examined it; it felt oily and foreign, leaving a slick residue that stained his fingertips. The sight was chilling: the hand curled around the throat in a death grip, as if trying to suffocate itself even in death.

Cole's heart drummed in his chest, a relentless rhythm that drowned out the hum of the city. He could feel the eyes of the police officers boring into him, their unease palpable as they lingered at the edges of the body, giving off an air of disgust and morbid curiosity. The heat from the late afternoon sun seeped into his skin, mingling with the metallic scent that twisted in his nostrils. He had learned to compartmentalize, but today was different; the dread was a live wire under his skin.

Joanne's voice pulled him back, sharp as shards of glass. "What do you see?" she asked, kneeling beside him, her brow furrowed as she examined the body. Cole sensed her keen focus yet wondered if she was using it to mask her aversion to the scene.

He inhaled deeply and forced clarity into his mind. "The ink," he murmured, barely above a whisper. "It is a deliberate choice." He felt the words tumble out, each syllable heavy with implication. "It's meant to convey something, like a signature or a message."

Joanne leaned closer, her expression sharpening as she processed his observations. "You think it's ritualistic?" she asked, her voice low yet laced with a hint of fascination mingled with discomfort. Cole felt an involuntary shiver run through him; the idea settled uncomfortably in his gut.

"More than that," he replied, tracing the outline of the inked symbol with a fingertip and feeling its slick surface. "This isn't random. It's orchestrated."

"Rituals can be orchestrated," Joanne said. "Voodoo or some other obscure practice. I have heard that sacrifice and body painting occur in certain cultures. This could be something like that."

Cole's gaze flickered back to the victim, the pallid skin contrasting sharply with the inky blackness that consumed her left hand. The implications gnawed at him, a relentless itch in the back of his mind. He straightened slightly, fighting against the wave of nausea rising within him. "This isn't something I'm familiar with, if it is a ritual. How familiar are you with those types of things?"

Joanne's brow furrowed deeper, and Cole could see her struggle between what she wanted to say and what she thought he wanted to hear. He interjected before she made that decision. "Joanne, if this is going to work, I need you to tell me what you are thinking. No modesty, no filter. Just your knowledge, instinct, and thought process. Please do not just tell me what you think I want to hear."

Her brow unfurrowed and her shoulders noticeably relaxed. Cole had not even noticed how much tension had gripped his new partner. She looked back down at the body. "The arrangement is too precise. The pose is too specific." She looked up into Cole's eyes. "I know a bit, but more importantly, I know people who would know about rituals of all types."

Cole noted how Joanne's demeanor shifted as she engaged with the scene. Once the tension left her shoulders, her analytical gaze bore down on the arrangement before them. He felt a flicker of relief; the push for honesty had been a gamble, but it seemed to have paid off.

"Let's find out who the victim is," he suggested, trying to steer their focus. The thought of digging into personal histories dulled the adrenaline that had been building through him.

While time-consuming and often thankless, tracking down the victim's name and finding each name associated with her could lead to a thread they needed to unravel. The victim lay there, a lifeless body for now, but within her identity could lie the key to understanding this macabre display.

Joanne nodded, her eyes still lingering on the ink as if it held secrets beyond comprehension. "I agree. We should get her identified. Then I can start reaching out to my contacts about any local religious groups that might connect," she replied, determination creeping back into her voice. "There are communities in Baltimore that delve into rituals; they have their own twisted interpretations of faith." Her voice held a peculiar blend of fascination and dread, much like a scholar drawn to forbidden knowledge. "This could be a message to someone. A warning, perhaps."

"That sounds good. We should clear out of the locals' way and let them bag her for the coroner. We can follow behind and meet the body there." Cole scribbled some notes in his pad, flipped it closed, and put it back in his jacket pocket before turning toward the door to leave.

Chapter 4

Smile Its Black Toothed Grin

The room felt chill, the harsh fluorescent lights painting everything in stark contrast. Cole stood by the figure on the autopsy table, a grotesque reminder of the darkness lurking within the city he had only just begun to navigate. The victim lay on a steel slab, naked, with her eyes open toward the heavens. As he scanned her body, his gut twisted at the sight of her contorted neck, flesh bruised and marred by deep indents that spoke of a brutal struggle against an overwhelming force. This was no ordinary murder; it was a statement, a show of intent.

The metallic scent of fresh blood mingled with something sweeter, more sinister: the faint aroma of ink. The victim's skin was pale, almost translucent, and as he leaned closer, he could see the intricate web of bruises encircling the neck. The victim's left hand bore the signature mark, a stark segment of black ink that seemed to pulse against the pale skin. Cole still did not understand how the ink stained the hand completely but left the neck devoid of any trace.

"Agent Hunter?" Hearing his name shook him from his concentrative state. The coroner, Dr. Samuel Hargrove, moved with the precision of a surgeon as Cole watched him walk into the room.

Hargrove's hair, peppered with gray, framed a face that had seen too much yet remained resolutely stoic. He wore thick glasses that magnified his eyes, giving them an almost insect-like quality: sharp and observant, missing nothing. When he leaned over the body draped on the cold steel table, his fingers moved deftly as they traced the contours of flesh and bone.

Cole and his partner, eager to get answers on the cause of death, paid close attention to the coroner's description of the victim's crushed windpipe. The killer had then poured ink down her throat to accompany the dyed left hand. The ink had coated the inside of her mouth. He surmised it had pooled in the back of her throat and slowly dripped down into her esophageal cavity, passing through the crushed windpipe like coffee dripping into a pot.

The coroner pulled out a notepad from his back pocket, lowered his glasses to the edge of his nose, squinted, and read. "Her ID says her name is Sarah Whitman. She was twenty-eight years old, an Episcopalian, and she was local. Unfortunately, her ID didn't give us any information other than that."

Cole shook the coroner's hand. "That is more than we had, Doc. Hopefully, the police get more information from her neighbors. I appreciate you doing a rush job on her."

The man shook Cole's hand in return and nodded as he walked away toward the desk on the other side of the room, apparently indicating that the briefing was over.

***

Back in the office, Cole leaned back in his chair, fingers tapping against the well-worn cover of his notebook. The dim light of the precinct flickered overhead, casting shadows across the cluttered desk. He could almost taste the stale cigarette smoke lingering in the air, mixed with the faint scent of sweat from a long night shift.

His partner's voice broke through his thoughts, animated yet tinged with frustration. "You think it's a religion or cult thing? Or do you think I am way off base?"

Cole leaned forward, his mind picturing the victim's mouth filling with the viscous black ink. "I can't rule it out, partner. It could be religious or ritualistic. We know it wasn't accidental, we know that. She wasn't killed by the ink being poured down her throat. That was postmortem. So, it was a message, a calling card, or a red herring. The killer could be leaving this as a calling card. Alternatively, it is part of some religious ceremony or ritual, the purpose of which we have absolutely no idea."

Cole tossed his notebook to the end of his desk and let out a sigh. "Any luck with your contacts in that area?"

"I reached out to everyone I thought could have some insight into this, and they all were just as puzzled as we are. There is no known ritual that involves all the components of the kill scene. This killer staged the body meticulously and used the black ink with intention. All of my contacts say that level of specificity sounds ritualistic, but it is not from any they have ever heard of."

Cole leaned forward, resting his forearms on the cool surface of his desk. "I think we need to understand what the ink means. Why the throat? Why the left hand? Why her?"

Joanne began to speak but was interrupted by the shrill ringing of the phone on her desk. She reached over, picked up the receiver, and placed it near her face. "This is Agent Misko." Her eyebrows rose sharply as she took in whatever was said on the other end of the line. "We will be on our way."

She quickly threw the phone toward the base and grabbed her jacket. "We have a new crime scene, and apparently it is definitely our guy."

*****

Cole stepped across the threshold as anticipation settled in his stomach like a stone. The kitchen was dim, illuminated only by the weak afternoon light filtering through grimy windows. He barely registered the musty smell clinging to the air until an undercurrent of rot hit him.

His gaze traveled reluctantly to the table, where the family sat. Their bodies were meticulously arranged, as if posed for a grotesque family portrait. The grins were contorted and surreal, almost cartoonish as they stretched impossibly wide. Blackened teeth glinted menacingly in the muted light, a stark contrast to their light-skinned faces.

Anger welled up inside Cole. This was no ordinary crime scene; it was an invitation, a taunt wrapped in dark ritual. The black teeth grinned back at him, a sickening mockery of joy. Each face appeared frozen in some twisted celebration, yet their lifeless eyes seemed to scream in muted agony.

Cole reached for his notebook but paused, his hand hesitating midair. He noticed the contrast of their serene positions; each member of the family held the hand of the person next to them. Each had their left hand dyed a deep, dark black, signaling to anyone in the know that only one person could be responsible for this.

The stillness in the room was oppressive. Half a dozen police officers were present, and not a single one dared to move or make a sound. Cole thought that was more out of fear than solemnity. The silence was broken only by the scratching of Joanne's pencil against her notebook as she feverishly jotted down everything she could see.

Cole looked up to the officers standing around and began issuing orders. "There has to be a thread connecting these victims and the other victim. I need you all to start digging around here for anything that could be a link. I need you to go door to door and show the picture of the first victim to the neighbors. Ask if they know her or if this family knows her."

The officers quickly began moving about, jarred from their previously reverent state into action. Cole leaned down and began observing the scene, searching for any clues that could be found.

Chapter 5

Lofty Ideals

He preferred to remember the arrangement of the Wilson family in idealized, near-sacred detail, replaying the scene in his mind as a composer might rehearse the grandest movement of a symphony, listening for the shimmer of every suspended note.

It had taken him no time at all to learn Mrs. Wilson's patterns and habits. It was a simple task to replace several food items in their kitchen with drugged versions while she was out running errands that day. After that, he simply had to wait for the family to eat and go to sleep, each of them unaware that they would never wake.

He moved through their home with reverence, orchestrating the tableau with a devotion to symmetry and symbolism that most would call madness, but which he, in the innermost sanctum of his mind, knew to be the highest form of art.

There was no hesitation, no improvisation; every movement had been determined in advance, mapped out in the hours he spent watching the family move through their ordinary lives, attuned to the subconscious patterns they themselves failed to notice.

The children came first, as was only appropriate. He carried them down from their bedrooms one at a time to the dining room. There, he arranged them gently at the table, hands folded over their chests, eyelids wide open in an appearance of mute terror.

The wife was next. He carried her to the table and arranged her arms at her sides, outstretched, one toward each of her children. He then gently placed each child's hand in their mother's. He had pried her eyes open and then, with more force than he had expected, opened her mouth into a frozen, jack-o'-lantern-like grin.

Only the husband was left. The man's weight made the final pose a technical challenge. The killer placed him opposite his wife and positioned him identically, his hands forever embracing those of his children. The killer quickly manipulated the man's eyelids and mouth to mirror the rest of the family. There was no need for theatrics beyond this; the simplicity of the arrangement was itself the message.

Then came the ink. Even now, he could recall the sensation of the black ink with its thick viscosity, the dark promise in its glint as he coated each left hand. Noting to himself that the smallest child's palm took hardly any effort to cover completely, he treated the application as ritual. It felt to him like it cemented the bodies in death. It was the most intimate moment of all: flesh bared, his steady hands staining their skin in a moment that would outlast everything else about them.

He took a moment to appreciate the beauty of consistency, the way the ink dried to an obsidian sheen, identical on every victim, a perfect signature. He did not smile at the beauty he created, though it might have been expected. This was not pleasure but fulfillment. The difference was everything.

He remembered also the silence: how the house, so recently filled with voices and routines, became as still as a mausoleum, save for the faintest echo of the city's pulse outside. He traced the perimeter of each room, observing the smallest items decorating them.

He left the house clean. He made certain of it, as he always did. There would be no careless hairs, no prints, no misplaced fibers. He moved through the aftermath like a ghost, double-checking his work. This was not like it had been in St. Louis. Forensics were getting better every single day. Chemical analysis and tool comparisons were now being introduced in the courtroom and winning cases. The Supreme Court had even disseminated the Federal Rules of Evidence, which allowed the smarter criminals to learn the rules and what to avoid.

After one last sweep of the home, he stepped out the back door and dispersed into the predawn light, unnoticed and unburdened. His only regret was that the world would see only the residue of his intention: the muddied secondhand accounts, the reduction of his design to headlines and a momentary shudder.

Later, he recalled the scene while he cleaned the ink brush with gentle, circular motions, mindful of contamination. He catalogued the details of the scene in his mind, refining his process for the next composition. He had already begun composing his next arrangement even before he had left the Wilsons' home. His mind worked over the details as he ran the water over his hands at the sink.

When he finally slept, he dreamed not of the Wilsons but of the one adversary he hoped would be worthy of his attention—the man who would eventually decipher the pattern and recognize the message. Hunter was the only real audience, the only one capable of seeing the intention behind the chaos.

He remembered how, in their previous encounter in St. Louis, he had had to resort to mailing evidence directly to Hunter to move the investigation forward.

He was certain that this time Agent Hunter would piece together the connections. The killer knew, with bone-deep certainty, that Hunter would recognize the significance of Jennifer Martinez's relationship with Michael Bennett and would immediately pursue the deeper connection to Mark Wilson, Bennett's best friend since their undergraduate years at Johns Hopkins.

The killer considered the possibility that, presented with the Wilsons' murder, Hunter might see the personal element as either too intentional or as a warning shot across the bow; perhaps he would admire the audacity, perhaps even interpret it as a challenge. Was it too obvious for a Bureau man who prided himself on cleverness, or was the link subtle enough to pass unnoticed?

He had a fondness for these dilemmas, for the little crises of self-doubt they triggered in men like Hunter. Men who believed they were playing one game when the real game was happening right in front of them, without their knowledge. Men who clung to the idea that human behavior could be reduced to a finite series of motives and outcomes. It was almost endearing how quickly even the best of them could be led astray by the suggestion of logic, by the lure of patterns so neat they must surely be a trap. Hunter's own psychology background, he thought, would probably lead to his ruin.

The killer lay on his back in his makeshift apartment, fingers interlaced on his chest, eyes tracing the cracks in the ceiling above, and wondered for the hundredth time whether Hunter would see through the surface to the deeper structure beneath, to the design that was both a confession and an accusation.

He debated, as he often did, whether he had overplayed his hand; perhaps the connections were too linear, too narratively satisfying for any investigator, even one as obtuse as Hunter. Still, there was pleasure in the risk. There was also the quiet, private satisfaction of knowing that, somewhere in the city's web of rowhouses and underground bars, an agent's mind would be running ragged trying to keep up with the unfolding story. A small mercy, he supposed, that the game was being played against someone worthy of it. He decided, finally, that the trail was neither too cold nor too hot; it would force Hunter to question his own sanity at least once before the end, which was all the killer really required.

He also thought he needed to revisit the timeline and the planning for his next moves, knowing the need to maintain momentum to keep the investigation moving in his desired direction. He would hate for Agent Hunter to think there was any moment of peace. No. The killer wanted Agent Hunter to feel that this was unrelenting and all-encompassing. Agent Hunter deserved nothing less.

Chapter 6
The Finding Out Phase

At precisely nine, the agents reassembled in the Bureau's cramped briefing room, where the details of the new case sprawled across corkboard and tile. The dim classroom lighting enhanced the sense of mourning that hovered above the table, which was itself littered with crime-scene photographs: the family of four, their faces obscured by evidence tags, and the table still set as if ready for a meal.

Along one wall, photographs of the first victim, the young woman in the floral dress, had been pinned as if waiting for a side-by-side that might finally conjure meaning. A thick hush filled the room.

The news had spread through the Bureau like wildfire, a grim shadow cast over the water-cooler chatter. Cole had felt it, the sharp edges of suspicion and whispered dread echoing through the sterile halls of the Baltimore Field Office. The case files piled high on his desk were more than a mere collection of evidence; they were a reminder of the ghosts that loomed in the air, their presence dense as fog.

He leaned back in his chair, fingers drumming against the cracked leather of his notebook, each tap resonating with the rhythm of his unease. The weight of unfinished business clung to him like a second skin. St. Louis had painted a vivid picture he couldn't shake, a slow-motion reel of decisions made and opportunities missed. He wished he could erase those images—the victims' faces smeared with confusion, their empty eyes pleading for resolution.

Director Johnson presided, sleeves rolled and tie already loosened, wearing the fatigue of a man whose sleep deficit ticked ever upward. He stabbed at his binder, summoning everyone's focus.

"All right, this is what we have: the Wilson family. Mother, father, and two young children. They died in their home sometime between eight and ten. Nothing was missing, no forced entry, no sign of struggle. Not a single neighbor saw or heard anything."

He let the first page of the binder hang as he flipped it. "The father worked as a line supervisor at the Harbor Shipyards. The mother was a part-time substitute at St. Therese Elementary. The daughter, only ten years old, was top of her class, and the son was only eight."

Agent Cole Hunter wrinkled his brow and hunched over his battered notepad. "Nothing stands out?"

"Nothing stands out," Johnson replied, voice flat. "They were about as ordinary as you get. No debts, no legal trouble, no affairs. The only notable thing is how absolutely unnotable they were."

Johnson flipped the last few pages, then closed the binder and brought it down onto the table. He rubbed the bridge of his nose before saying, "No apparent connection between the family and our original victim."

Joanne sat at the edge of the group, arms folded tightly. "The first victim," she said, gesturing at the pinned photograph, "Sarah Whitman. No connection to the Wilson family?"

"None that we can find," Johnson said. "She was a college student, lived alone, worked at a bookstore. Not even the same church. Not even on the same side of the city."

Cole's pen hovered above the page. "So what's the link? We have two scenes, two sets of victims, totally different backgrounds, no overlap in routine."

"That's what we're here to find out," Johnson said, rapping his knuckles against the table. "For now, our only constant is the method. No witnesses, rapid and silent, and whoever did this is getting bolder."

They fell into contemplative silence, each running through the permutations of motive and means while the evidence boards watched on, inscrutable.

A sudden commotion at the door startled them. An agent Hunter did not recognize came rushing in with a thick file and said, "I think I have a suspect!"

"Well, please feel free to share with the rest of us, Agent Da Lay," Johnson said, leaning forward in anticipation and irritation.

Agent Da Lay paled slightly. "I had been contacting surviving family members of the family that died and showing the picture of the first victim to see if anyone recognized her. The sister of the father in the family recognized her. Apparently, she was the father's best friend's girlfriend."

"Did you happen to get the best friend's name?" Johnson asked irritably.

"Yes, sir." Agent Da Lay clumsily handed the folder to Director Johnson, who took a few moments to thumb through the first pages before passing it to Agent Hunter.

"You two get over to this address now. We will have units standing by with a freshly signed warrant in hand," Johnson barked at Cole and Joanne.

"You got it, Director," Cole said as he grabbed the folder. Cole and Joanne rose and headed quickly for the door.

"Agents, do not screw this up. Wait for the warrant and then get our man. I want this to be bulletproof. Do you hear me?" Johnson said, somehow even gruffer than before.

Both agents nodded as they left.

Chapter 7

Salutations From The Grave

The house, a narrow row nestled in Waverly's residential web, looked as if it had not been lived in for long. Cole and Misko eyed the edges of the porch for signs of recent disturbance—muddy prints, a misplaced planter's shard—before knocking. The man who opened the door, Michael Bennett, had the pallor and posture of someone dragged away from actuarial tables rather than sleep. His eyes pinged between the two agents, first in confusion, then assessing.

Cole introduced himself to Mr. Bennett and informed him they were federal agents, flashing badges. "We'd like to ask a few questions," he said, his voice flat and intended to give nothing away.

Bennett nodded, but he did not step aside to invite them in. Instead, he lingered in the doorway as if, by sheer presence, he might keep their questions outside.

"We're hoping you can help us identify someone," Misko said, producing the autopsy photo of the first victim. She was cleaned up, but the image was unmistakably clinical.

Bennett took one look and recoiled, his hand rising fast to his mouth, then lowering with forced control. "That's… oh God, that's my girlfriend," he said, voice already flecked with panic. "Sarah. She left three days ago… she was driving to visit her family in

Chicago. I hadn't heard from her, and I…" He trailed off, eyes growing glassy, and Cole watched the man's hands start to tremble.

"Did you have any contact with her after she left?" Cole asked, softening just enough so the question would not sound like an accusation.

"No. I mean, she said she would call me from her parents when she arrived, but then nothing." Bennett's voice faltered. "I thought maybe she got busy and forgot, or…" He suddenly seemed acutely aware of his own dishevelment, pulling at his shirt collar. "Can you tell me what happened?"

"We're still piecing it together," Misko said, her tone betraying practiced ambiguity. "Do you mind if we come inside?"

Bennett hesitated, then stepped back, ushering them into a sparsely furnished living room. The agents took in the environment: a cluttered desk crowded with stacks of disorganized papers, random dirty clothes scattered across the hardwood, a half-empty mug calcified with days-old coffee. On the wall, a chalkboard littered with equations.

"You'll have to forgive the mess. I am an accountant, and this is my busy time of year."

Cole ignored Mr. Bennett's comment and began to steer the conversation gently. "Had she mentioned any trouble? Anyone who might have wanted to hurt her?"

"No, nothing," Bennett said. "Sarah was… everyone loved her. She worked at the library. She didn't… I mean, this can't be real." His breathing came short, on the verge of hyperventilation.

"Was she acting strangely before she left? Did she have any fears, any enemies?" Misko pressed.

Bennett shook his head. "No. She was excited to see her family. That's all."

There was a silence, measured and heavy, that Cole let linger. Then he asked, "Mr. Bennett, are you aware of what happened to your best friend's family?"

The question landed with a thud. Bennett blinked, blank, caught mid-pace. "What… what do you mean?"

The two agents, their faces a careful mask of professional detachment, motioned for the man to sit. He perched on the edge of his sofa, hands trembling. They laid out the photographs on the low table between them: one, the likeness of the woman he'd just named as his girlfriend; the next, grotesquely altered, her face slack and her left hand inked black, the details mercifully blurred by the poor quality of the crime-scene print.

He stared at the array as if he did not recognize the images. "I don't understand," he said at last, voice thin and papery, each word sapping his strength. "She was going to visit her family. She said she'd call when she got in. Are you sure—"

Misko, standing in the kitchen doorway to block any exit, directed the conversation with the probing detachment of a surgeon. "That's not all," she said, sliding a folder across the table.

Inside were other photos: of his best friend's family. Father first, then the mother, then the two young children, all bearing the now-familiar black ink radiating from their left palms.

"This happened yesterday. You were identified as a close acquaintance."

Agent Hunter tilted the photos to better catch the afternoon light, exposing the glossy sheen of the developing fluid under the dim lighting of the room. "Mr. Bennett, do you have any reason to believe the Wilsons were in danger? When did you last see any of them?"

The man's jaw went slack. His knuckles whitened against the fabric of his pants as if bracing for impact. He shook his head slowly, then with mounting urgency, hands up in a pantomime of surrender. "I haven't seen him in weeks. We had a falling out, a stupid argument at the bar—nothing serious. You can ask around. Last night? Last night I was home."

Misko scribbled notes in a small spiral-bound pad, her pencil scratching like insect legs across the paper. "We'll verify your timeline. In the meantime, we'll need you to stay in town. No trips. No visitors. If you need to reach us, call us directly." She produced a business card, crisp and uncreased, and set it atop the morgue-fresh image, an incongruous touch of bureaucracy amid carnage.

The man nodded mutely, as if any more words might summon something worse.

The agents let themselves out, closing the door with heavy finality. On the porch, the dying afternoon cast long shadows over the rowhouses, the city's hum growing denser as workers returned home and porch lights flickered on in anticipation of darkness. Two police cruisers were parked in front with four officers in ready positions. Cole motioned for them to stand down.

Misko exhaled through her teeth, her composure slipping just enough for Cole to notice the tension held in her shoulders.

"Thoughts?" Cole asked, breaking the silence.

"He's either the best actor I've ever seen, or he really doesn't have a clue," Misko said. "But the connections don't lie. He's the common denominator. If he's not doing the deed, someone's getting lucky with a convenient patsy."

Cole glanced back at the window, where the silhouette of the man was now half-concealed by a hastily drawn curtain. "Still, it doesn't fit the profile. Our guy's meticulous. This guy can barely keep it together. But until there is something better, he's all we've got."

Misko grunted agreement and pulled a cigarette from her coat pocket. "I'll tell the local police they need an unmarked unit to sit on his house. If he bolts, we know he's hiding something."

They crossed the lawn, the grass bristling with the day's accumulated static, and slid into the government sedan. As they drove off, Cole watched the rearview mirror, half-expecting the target to come sprinting after them, but the house remained shuttered in dread.

Chapter 8

On The Turning Away

Cole's phone screamed him awake at 2:34 a.m., its shrill insistence slicing through his uneasy sleep and rattling the glass of water on his nightstand. He fumbled for it, not wanting it to wake Shayla, nearly smacking it onto the floor before he managed to answer.

The voice on the other end delivered the words in a rush. "Agent Hunter? Baltimore PD shadowed the suspect from the Fell's Point waterfront all the way to a derelict row house west of the viaduct."

Cole rubbed his still sleep-filled eyes with one hand as he listened and looked over Shayla's still sleeping form.

"They had eyes on him the whole way. The police observed when the suspect went inside at approximately one-thirty and have reported that nobody's come or gone since."

Cole swung his legs over the edge of the mattress, adrenaline purging the last wisps of sleep from his bloodstream. He dressed hurriedly, mind racing as he replayed the details of the last forty-eight hours in his head. He did not like the escalating pace, the meticulous staging, the possible religious undertones.

He paused only to scribble a note for Shayla that read *At a potential crime scene. Could be awhile. Love you.* After placing the note on the refrigerator, he was out the door and into the stinging night air.

Misko was already at the scene when Cole arrived, her silhouette hard and angular in the yellow gaze of the streetlamps. They conferred briefly with the perimeter officers, who had cordoned off the row house and were keeping a nervous distance. Cole could feel the anxiety rolling off them in waves.

He and Misko drew their weapons and went in. The front door yielded with a groan, and the foyer offered up a noticeable stench of rot and mildew. They advanced down the narrow hallway, boots crunching on debris, and entered a living area stripped bare except for a single standing lamp with a green banker's shade.

In this almost empty room, they found Mr. Bennett cradling a young woman in his arms as though she might wake at any moment.

The scene was almost tender, and for one brief instance Cole thought he was looking at a father comforting a sleeping daughter. But the girl's head lolled at a grotesque angle, her face mottled blue and purple, black ink staining around her mouth, and her left hand stained to the wrist in the same patent-leather black that marked all the killer's victims.

As Cole registered the unfolding scene in front of him, he saw at Mr. Bennett's feet a sizeable vat, the kind you'd buy at a hardware store, two-thirds full of thick, viscous ink.

Misko advanced first, gun aimed at Bennett's head. Her voice was surprisingly gentle. "FBI. Mr. Bennett, put your hands where I can see them, please."

The silence following her words hung in the air for what seemed like an impossible time as Mr. Bennett did not move. His gaze floated above the girl's corpse. The look on his face was unfocused and appeared confused, as if he were waiting for the next line of a script he had practiced but forgotten.

The dead woman's head lolled against his chest, hair matted together from a mixture of sweat, her left hand marbled to the wrist in a dense lacquer. The effect was less like a murder scene and more like an unfinished painting, as if they were frozen in a surreal nightmare.

Cole noticed a spattering of ink ran down the inside of Bennett's forearm, bisecting the blue veins, and pooled in the crook of his elbow. He looked up, blinking once at Cole, then at Misko, as if they had interrupted a tender moment, not a grotesque rite.

"She is so quiet," he murmured, voice papery thin. "Why is she so quiet?"

Misko holstered her gun and approached Bennett. They got him to his feet with minimal resistance, but Cole noted the tremor in Bennett's legs and the near catatonia that had replaced whatever confusion had been present there. He saw the man's eyes, wide and wet, reflecting the green glow of the lamp. There was no emotion, only a bone-deep flatness that made Cole shiver.

Cole had the uniforms sweep the rest of the house to ensure no one else was on the premises while Misko radioed for the forensics unit and watched Bennett as if he might collapse or burst into flames at any second.

Cole knelt by the girl's body, careful not to disturb the spatter of ink or the position of her limbs. Her palm was open, and her fingers were curled in a gesture so ordinary it made the atrocity harder to process. The ink across her mouth was deliberate, and the violence beneath was unmistakable.

Cole wondered, suddenly, how long it had taken her to die and if Bennett had watched the entire time. The thought left him shaken.

*****

Only once she was zipped into a body bag and the house filled with shuffling evidence techs did they walk Bennett outside. His hands were cuffed, his head bowed, as he passed the glut of police officers and the flashing blue and red lights from the patrol cars cascading up and down the sleeping street.

Cole stared at the street as Bennett was loaded into the back of a squad car. The victory felt hollow. The ink, the careful staging, the dead girl in his arms—these were all pieces of evidence that pointed decisively at their suspect, but Cole could not shake the sensation that it was all too easy. The whole thing lacked reasoning and felt illogical.

He glanced at Misko, who was already on the car radio, presumably alerting the chain of command and quietly accepting the congratulations that would soon come pouring in. To her, this was a clean bust, a meticulous execution of their professional obligation, the case sewn up with surgical precision. She even allowed herself a rare, weary smile as she lit a cigarette, her posture loose and disarmed for the first time since he had met her.

"Hey," she said, flicking her lighter and exhaling a thin plume of smoke, "you should enjoy this, Cole. We just closed out the most notorious case in the eastern corridor. You know what that means? Commendations. Promotions, even."

There was a brightness in her eyes, the kind that came from relief and adrenaline, but also a hunger for the validation that their line of work almost never provided.

Cole tried to mirror her satisfaction, but the smile would not come. "Yeah," he said quietly. "I guess we did."

He watched the other officers as they milled about, some crowding for a glimpse of the suspect, others already swapping war stories and predictions for tomorrow's headlines. The block, once an anonymous swath of broken brick and buckled asphalt, would now be immortalized in the annals of police work.

But Cole's mind kept returning to the look in Bennett's eyes— the dissonant flat stare, the way his hands trembled when the girl was finally taken from his grasp. It felt all wrong.

"I'm telling you, Cole," Misko said, reading the unfinished thought in his face. "You're overthinking it. Sometimes people are just broken. Sometimes it's not about the puzzle or the pattern. Sometimes the story is exactly what it looks like."

Cole reluctantly gave her a reassuring smile and a quick nod. They waited for the crime scene unit to finish their sweep, then wrote up their initial statements on the trunk of a cruiser.

Above them, the city lights diffused in a haze of sodium yellow, and somewhere in the distance, a late-night freight train sounded its mournful horn. Cole felt a creeping exhaustion settle into his bones, the kind that no amount of sleep or caffeine would cure.

He stole another look at the house, at the thin slit of green still leaking through the window from that damned banker's lamp. He wondered, absurdly, if anyone would turn off the light, or if the echo of what they had found inside would just burn on, unblinking, until someone finally leveled the place.

By the time they returned to headquarters, the phones had already started ringing. Reporters. Supervisors. The Bureau's own press office. Cole and Misko were summoned for a preliminary debrief with the Assistant Special Agent in Charge, who kept his gratitude crisp and reserved. The man congratulated them both with a handshake and a promise that the "good work done here tonight would not go unnoticed."

There was talk of a news conference, but Cole just wanted to be back in his bed next to Shayla.

He began the paperwork immediately, the first step in finalizing any case. Misko powered through the forms with steadfast efficiency, while Cole found himself staring at the lines and boxes, unable to keep focused on completing even the most basic fields without replaying the last few hours in detail. He wrote and rewrote his account, each time hoping that if he looked at it from a new angle, the thing that was bothering him would finally come into focus.

It never did.

He stared at the clock, then at the blank wall, then at the paperwork again.

He felt in his gut that there should be more to this.

Chapter 9

The Birds Win

Camden Yards filled with the sound of birdsong and bellows, a city's restless energy boiling over into the stands as the Baltimore Orioles eked out their ninth-inning miracle. The stadium erupted in orange and black as the team beat the National League Champion Cincinnati Reds.

On the field, the players bounded toward home plate with the manic glee of men who understood just how temporary this victory would be. In the stands, fathers lifted children overhead, and strangers slapped each other's backs as though the wind had shifted in their favor for the first time in decades.

Miles from the field, Mr. Bennett sat at a different kind of plate, under the cold scrutiny of fluorescent lights and institutional walls. He wore a suit, a tie, and a second skin of dread as the jury announced their verdict.

To Cole, who sat in the back of the court, the setting felt eerily familiar. He thought it would probably feel that way to anyone who remembered the St. Louis incident, that trial that had ended quickly, just as this one had.

Cole noticed that the air felt thick with the inevitability of it all. He had watched, from the safety of newsprint and distance, as the last defendant's life was dissected and judged. He had only been present for the single hour he needed to testify, and now once again for the verdict.

The presiding judge read off the accusations in a voice stripped of emotion and devoid of clues as to the verdict. The words were less a list of sins and more a recitation of significant cruelties.

Wearing his suit, heart rattling, Mr. Bennett awaited the sentence. All the while, a part of him clung to the faint hope that the world outside the courthouse might somehow intercede. But the ritual played on, and the laws of man came down swiftly.

The verdict came: guilty on all counts. As in St. Louis, the sentencing of death by execution followed from the judge with an ease that was unsettling to Cole.

***

The killer had somehow gotten bored. He blamed himself. His meticulous plan to frame Mr. Bennett was originally intended to last much longer. But after he had staged the family, the killer felt the shine wear off the project.

This led him to immediately accelerate the plan. He phoned Mr. Bennett and told him his girlfriend's sister wished to meet him immediately and that he should go to the row house. The girl had already been killed and staged, and Bennett had exquisitely taken the bait. To the killer's delight, Bennett went into shock and froze there.

The killer did not have to wait long for the police and agents to arrive and bring about the endgame. While the shine had worn off, the killer still received that rush he was looking for when he saw Cole walking Bennett out in cuffs. The killer knew he had won.

Unexpectedly, he saw something in Cole's eyes and demeanor he had not expected. There was a distinct lack of satisfaction, a hesitation. This was later confirmed when Cole testified at trial. There was no conviction in his voice. He recited facts but put no emotion behind them.

Had Agent Hunter finally caught on? Was the game about to get more interesting? The killer had not anticipated this development. Cole was just a tool, a useful idiot. Perhaps a muse, if the killer was being generous. This new twist opened up a world of possibilities.

The killer had donned his priest attire and given Mr. Bennett his last rites, just as he had previously in St. Louis. Yes, he admitted he was still elated when he revealed to him why he was targeted and framed, and yes, he still smiled while Bennett was strapped into the electric chair. But this all felt like foreplay now. The game was going to change. Now that Agent Hunter was wising up, there was going to be a whole new level to explore.

As the killer walked away from the prison after the execution, he smiled to himself as the beginnings of his new game began to take shape inside his mind. Oh, Agent Hunter was about to really regret having caught an inkling of what was going on. The killer was going to make sure of it.

Chapter 10
The Proposal

After the verdict, the city pulsed with the thrum of a home team victory and the quiet, hard-won satisfaction of justice delivered. Inside a cramped corner booth at a Fell's Point tavern, the Bureau's finest squeezed in elbow-to-elbow under the haze of hanging lanterns, the smell of spilled beer and fried onions thick enough to taste.

Cole, still in the suit he had worn to the courthouse, sat with one arm draped around Shayla's shoulders and the other raised in a crude imitation of a champagne toast, though the glass he held was filled with nothing more glamorous than tap water. Misko and two junior agents hunched over the center of a nearby table. The junior agents were listening in rapt attention as she regaled them with whose hunch had been closest to the truth and who really was the reason the case got cracked.

There was relief in the room, but it was the brittle kind. Like a pressure valve cracked open after months of building up steam, everyone knew the pressure would soon begin building again.

For Cole, the victory felt more like a reprieve than a triumph. He watched Shayla's profile as she laughed at something Misko said to the junior agents, her hair tucked behind her ear in the way it always was. Cole knew he should be happy they had made it through this case, despite the odds, despite the body count, and despite his own gnawing doubt. He felt the beginnings of a smile creep up, awkward and guilty at first.

When he grabbed Shayla's hands in his, she turned and immediately locked eyes with him, a warm smile gracing her lips.

"Shayla," he said, his voice dry from the stress of the day and his brow furrowing, "will you marry me?"

For a moment, Shayla's mouth worked wordlessly. Then she leaned in closely and kissed Cole passionately. When she paused and pulled back, Cole quizzed her, "I take it that is a yes?"

She giggled and said, "Of course it is a yes."

Cole kissed her again and thought to himself that this was what mattered. Not the case, not the Bureau, and definitely not the uneasy feeling that had been sitting with him since he arrested Mr. Bennett.

Shayla had said yes, and that was all that really mattered. Cole continued to kiss her, and for that brief instant the world was reduced to the two of them and the promise of a bright future.

From behind the polished mahogany, the bartender poured two shots of top-shelf bourbon and sent the waitress over to their table with them. Cole looked confused and glanced over at the bartender questioningly.

"On the house," he said, his gaze lingering, "for the happy fiancés."

Misko, having heard the bartender, immediately jumped up, glass in hand, and cheered. "Congratulations, partner!"

The whole bar erupted in congratulations, and Cole immediately forgot about the bartender as he was inundated with well-wishers.

Later, as the revelry thinned and Baltimore's shadows grew long in the window glass, Cole noticed a black smudge on his left hand that resembled a streak of ink. Was that deliberate, or was he just being paranoid?

He shook it off as paranoia and turned to thank the bartender, but the bar was empty.

THE END